RAPUNZEL'S
GUIDE
TO ALL THINGS
BRAVE
CREATIVE
&
FUN

First Hardcover Edition, September 2017 10 9 8 7 6 5 4 3 2 1

ISBN 978-1-4847-8726-7

Library of Congress Control Number: 2017941673

FAC-008598-17202

Printed in the United States of America

For more Disney Press fun, visit www.disneybooks.com

Designed by Gegham Vardanyan

RAPUNZEL'S GUIDE

TO ALL THINGS

BRAVE CREATIVE

& FUN

Written by SUZANNE FRANCIS
Illustrated by ENRIC PRAT

DISNEP PRESS
Los Angeles • New York

Contents

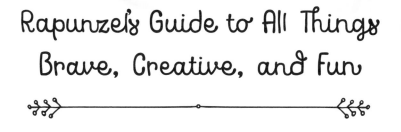

Rapunzel's Guide to All Things Brave, Creative, and Fun

So, you may have heard about me. I'm Rapunzel, the long-lost princess who was basically trapped in a tower for, well, a really long time. But now I'm free, so yay! Back in the tower, even though I stayed super busy doing fun things, like painting, playing chess, and reading books, my new life outside the tower has been more amazing than I ever could have imagined.

It's probably no surprise that, after being cooped up in a tower for so many years, I am totally in love with the outdoors, which is why I spend as much time as I can out in nature. But now that I'm back to being the princess of Corona, there's this whole long list of proper royalty-ish stuff I'm supposed to learn, and to be honest, a lot of it is pretty awkward. I mean, curtsying? I'm not sure if I'll ever get it right. But lucky for me, I still get to do some of the things I love, such as painting, and some things I've never tried before, like fencing. I just want to do and see and explore it all!

Of course, I can't resist the opportunity to put my own unique spin on things. Because, after all, doing things the ordinary way is highly overrated. I encourage you to do the same. Take these activities as inspiration and run with them (shoes are optional). Be brave as you venture out into the world! And if you ever feel for a moment that you're not ready for a life filled with adventure, creativity, and fun, just remember . . . there is always more in you!

Painting and Creating

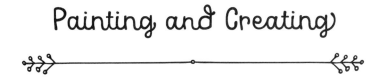

Painting! It's one of my favorite things to do! You know what's so great about painting? There are absolutely no rules that can't be broken. There's no such thing as a right way or a wrong way to paint, and anyone can do it. And I should know, since I've been painting every surface I could get my brush on—and come to think of it, breaking the rules—for as long as I can remember. To paint, all you need is a few basic supplies and something that inspires you. I find inspiration everywhere—a pretty flower, a colorful sunrise, Pascal's adorable little green (or blue, depending on his mood) face. . . . So just look around. Find something that inspires you. Then grab a brush and give painting a try—and don't be afraid to color outside the lines!

INSPIRATION

READY, SET, PAINT

Once you have your basic supplies together, you're ready to paint. Start simple and just have fun. Feel free to use a pencil to sketch things out first, or just dip your brush into paint and begin! As you paint, if you feel like you've made a mistake, don't be too quick to scrap your work and start over. One of the great things about art is that you can adjust things as you go. Simply paint something new over the part you don't like or blend parts together to form new shapes or designs. Sometimes what you think is a mistake ends up making your painting even better.

For something different, try making your own paintbrush using bundles of pine branches. The pine needles will create a unique texture on your painting. Collect some branches and bundle them together. Once you have the thickness you want, tie them together with a piece of string or wire. Tie them as tightly as possible so the branches don't slip out while you paint. Other natural materials like leaves, flowers, and twigs can make interesting paintbrushes as well.

If you don't have any paint on hand, brightly colored fruits, vegetables, and spices can be mashed and mixed up to create unique paint.

Always cover your work area and wear a smock or apron. Natural colors can stain, just like regular paint.

Homemade Paint

To make blueberry paint, mash up the blueberries and strain them, or ask a parent to help you by boiling them for a few minutes. If you'd like your paint to be thicker, add a little flour to the mixture.

For paint made from beets, spinach, carrots, and pomegranate seeds, you'll have to boil the ingredients to soften them before mashing and straining them.

To make paint using spices like cinnamon and turmeric, simply put the spices in a jar and mix in a little water.

I like using things like blueberries, beets, and pomegranate seeds. Once, I ran out of paint, so I grabbed a bunch of blueberries and smooshed them up in my hand. Then I used my fingers to paint. Okay, my fingers were kind of purple for a day or two, but the color that made it onto the paper was beautiful and bright!

Murals

Wall murals are some of my favorite things to paint. And lucky for me, the castle has plenty of huge walls that are just perfect for murals. Painting a mural is kind of like creating an entire life-size scene that I can imagine myself walking right into. How fun!

1: Clean and Prep

Check with your parents or guardians before painting a wall. Once you get approval for the space, look at the wall you're going to paint. Clean it up as much as you can so you have a clear, fresh space to work with. It's a good idea to paint a solid light color, like white, to create a blank canvas before starting your mural. If you don't have access to a wall that you can paint, create a mural on an old sheet or a large piece of fabric.

2: Secure the Area

Make sure everyone around you knows you're painting the space. It might be a good idea to put up a sign or a rope to mark it so that nobody leans against the wet paint.

I wish I had known about this little tip before I painted my last mural, because that is *exactly* how Eugene ended up with a lopsided pink flower smudged on the back of one of his favorite shirts. Whoops!

3: Step Back

Take a break and step back every now and then to check out your painting. Look at your mural from different angles. You'll be surprised by how different it looks, and it can help you make choices about things you may want to add or change.

Hair Art

Question: What would you do if you used to have miles and miles of magical hair but then you lost it . . . and then, suddenly, you got it all back again?

Well, after trying to hide it from everyone by piling it up on top of your head in a really fancy (but super-heavy and precarious) updo, you'd probably use it to create! That's what I like to do, anyway.

I have to admit, as much as I liked my perky, fun short hair, I'm pretty excited to be reunited with my long locks. I really enjoy finding different ways to put it up or back or to the side. . . . One of my go-tos is braiding, because, let's face it, it's basically a necessity. I mean, what would *you* do with all this hair? The great thing about braiding is that it is really simple to do and it's so versatile! Once you get the basics down, you can be really creative!

First, divide the hair you want to braid into three even sections. You'll want to keep these three sections divided the whole time you're braiding, so use your fingers to keep them separate.

You can start braiding with either of the outside pieces. Try starting with the left side. Take the left section and cross it over the one in the middle, swapping the left and center sections. Now grab the right section and cross it over the section in the center (the one that used to be the left section). Keep the pattern going, left section over the center, then right section over the center, and your braid will start to take shape.

Keep going until your braid is the length you want, and then tie it with something like a hair band, a clip, or a piece of ribbon.

Fancy Braids

Once you have the standard braid down, try the fishtail braid. It's simple, but it does take a bit longer, so be patient and make sure you have a little extra time. With the fishtail, instead of starting with three sections of hair, you start with two. The weaving is basically the same, but the third section of hair comes from the outside half of the two sections. So even though you're using two sections of hair, you make the third sections by splitting the two sections each and every time you bring it over.

I just love braiding Maximus's hair. I think it makes him look
so handsome! Once I wove apple blossoms into his tail and—I kid
you not—I could smell the sweet scent every time he swished his
tail around.

"You can use your new braiding skills to braid other things, too. Once I learned to braid, I started doing it with just about everything I could bend! I even braided a plate of spaghetti once—it was delish!

A French braid is kind of like the fishtail, but it gets slowly woven into the rest of the hair. Start with only a section of your hair divided into three pieces and slowly bring more and more hair into the outside pieces as you braid.

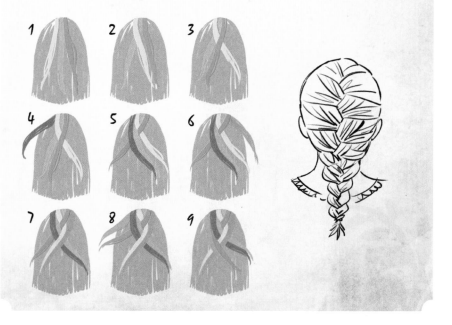

Try braiding things like yarn, flower stems, or vines to make bracelets, anklets, or even headbands. Check out these cute friendship bracelets Cassandra and I made for each other by braiding ribbon and thread.

The Art of Archery

Archery is tons of fun, but to be honest, my skills are pretty basic.
I'm still working on finding my true style, which is a big part of the
fun! But my best friend, Cassandra, is the real archery expert.

CASSANDRA'S ARCHERY LESSON

Okay, so you'll need to pick up a few things before getting started. I'm guessing you can gather that you will need a bow and some arrows, but it's also nice to have a quiver—that's a little pouch for your arrows that fits around your body for easy access. Be sure to pick up some protective gear as well, like an arm guard (also called a "bracer") for your bow arm (so you don't get slapped by the bowstring), a chest protector, and a shooting glove or a finger tab, which is just a small piece of fabric or leather that protects your drawing fingers.

You'll also want to do a little digging and find a local range that has targets for you to practice on. You can't just go shooting arrows in your backyard or at some park, because you could really hurt somebody. And as fun as it might sound to shoot an apple off your best friend's head, it's definitely not a good idea. You'll need to put in some good practice hours using a plain old target.

Now that you have all that together, you're probably itching to get started! But hold on—don't pick up that bow and arrow just yet. Think about it: you're going to try to hit a tiny little

point with another tiny little point. So read all the steps before giving it a try. Trust me on this.

I'm going to present the steps for right-handed archers, so if you're left-handed, just flip it.

➤➤➤ STEP 1 ➤
STANCE

Your stance is how you stand when you shoot your arrow. Even though it might seem strange, your stance has a lot to do with where your arrow ends up when you release it. You actually use your whole body to get the arrow to go to the precise spot you're aiming for.

Imagine a straight line drawn from your target all the way to where you are standing, and point your toes toward that line. Your left shoulder should be pointed toward your target. Got it? Okay. Now make sure your feet stay firmly planted about shoulder width apart.

Your upper body should be relaxed but strong. Hold the bow in your left hand. Now you're ready to reach for your first arrow.

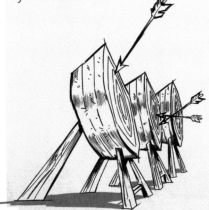

➤➤➤ STEP 2 ➤
NOCK THE ARROW

"Nocking the arrow" is just a fancy way of saying you're going to load the arrow onto the bow. The "nock" is the little notch in the top of the arrow that helps keep it from wobbling around on you while you're trying to shoot it. Place the nock into the bowstring. So how do you do that? Point the bow down toward the ground, and with the feather side of the arrow closest to you, place the arrow on the rest by your left hand. Slide the nock into the bowstring. Congratulations! Throw yourself a party. You've nock'd your first arrow.

➤➤➤ STEP 3 ➤
HOOK THE BOWSTRING

Now that your arrow is ready to go, it's time to put your fingers into position. Focus on three fingers on your right hand—your index, middle, and ring fingers. Place your index finger above the nock and the other two below. It can be tough, but try to keep the rest of your hand relaxed and focus only on those three fingers. I know you're probably excited to pull back and let an arrow fly, but hold on . . . there's more.

>>>— STEP 4 —➤

RAISE AND DRAW THE BOW

Keep your eyes on your target and raise your left arm up to shoulder height, straight out toward the target. Your elbow should be parallel to the ground. And no, don't use your foot. (Sorry, Raps.) Keep both of those firmly planted to help anchor your body. While you're raising the bow, try not to raise or hunch your shoulders. You want to keep your entire body as relaxed as possible.

Now, using your right hand, slowly pull the bowstring and your arrow back to where it feels comfortable to you—

somewhere between your chin and your ear. Keep that tension and pause for a moment as you check to make sure you've got everything right. . . . Are you good? Great. It's go time.

>>>— STEP 5 —➤

LET IT FLY

Keep your eyes on your target and release your arrow. Push your fingers out of the way as you let go of the arrow. Continue to hold the bow for a moment as you watch the arrow. Hopefully, it sinks into your target. If not, whatever. Just start at the beginning and try again.

Write On!

My mother gave me my first diary, and it has become one of my favorite things. What I love most about it is that it's not just words on a page. I also like to draw or paint in my diary to record experiences or feelings I've had. Later, I can spend hours flipping through the pages and remembering those experiences. I think everyone should have a diary! Don't you?

TEN JOURNALING TIPS FROM QUEEN ARIANNA

1   Try to find a quiet, comfortable place to make your entries so you can write without interruption.

2   Write as much or as little as you want, but keep it honest.

3   Write often. It is fine if you do not write every day, but make an effort to write *almost* every day.

4   Keeping a diary is all about you. Write as yourself.

5   Any experience is worth writing about. Write about places you go, people you meet, things you see, smell, hear, touch, and taste.

6 Your thoughts are precious. They are the little keys to discovering things about yourself that you might not know yet. Include them!

7 Carry your diary with you when possible. If you can't carry it with you, keep it in a safe place so you'll never lose it.

8 If you can't think of anything to write, try sitting for a moment and just letting your mind wander. Try starting your entry with "Today I . . ." and fill in the blank.

9 Entries do not have to be long—it's perfectly fine to write a few simple words to describe how you're feeling.

10 Be creative with your diary—your entries don't always have to be the same. Draw a picture of your feelings, write a poem, or make up a song. Even a simple thing like color adds a lovely touch to an entry, so keep colored pencils or paints handy.

My favorite tip is number 10. Creativity will help you make your diary whatever you want it to be. When I look back on pages I've filled, some of my favorite things are the drawings and paintings inside. They bring back such clear memories! Sometimes I'll even add things from the places my friends and I have explored, like the pretty flower and the lucky four-leaf clover I found in the hills behind the castle.

Nature's Palette

In case you haven't noticed, I spend a lot of time outside in nature. And there's plenty of nature around me . . . even inside the walls of Corona. My friends and I have so much fun creating art with the natural things we find. Try heading outside. Whether you're in a forest or a meadow, or by a lake or a stream, look around and see what you can create! With all the natural supplies, the possibilities are endless!

COLLECTING SUPPLIES

Just like getting ingredients together before baking a cake, you'll need to go outside and search for natural materials before creating natural art. Once you start looking, you'll be surprised by how much you can find. Go into your backyard or head to a nearby park or nature trail. Remember to bring a bag or a bucket to fill, and begin your search.

Pascal likes stacking things to see how high he can go. Sometimes we have a contest to see who can build a higher tower. Pascal is a tough little rascal to beat, though. He is extremely talented at keeping things balanced!

Mosaics are works of art made by putting little pieces together. They can be interesting patterns or complete pictures. Some artists use things like tiles or beads to make a mosaic, but you can also use things you find in nature.

First, collect your materials. Find things like twigs, leaves, seeds, stones, rocks, and flowers. Keep objects separated into piles so you can see what you have. It's a good idea to group them by color—so all the green objects will be in one section and all the gold objects will be in another, like a painter's palette.

Next, find some space for your mosaic and start creating. You can choose a subject first or just start setting things down and see what happens.

For the Love of Mud

I have to say, when I first met mud . . . it was love at first sight. This stuff is A-mazing! And it's always there, just waiting for you to jump in and play with it. Love love love mud! While my friends don't *completely* understand my feelings toward mud, they do enjoy creating mud creatures. We use mud like clay and make our own creatures, then decorate them with sticks, pebbles, and other things. When you add those details, they really seem to come to life.

TREE FACES

Use mud and a few other found objects to give a tree a face. First, take some mud and form it into the shape of a head. Then press it against the side of a tree. (You can also make a face on the side of a fallen log, a tree stump, or even the forest floor.)

Next, collect things to use for the features. Try using stones for eyes, seeds for teeth, and leaves for hair. Scout around and see what you can find.

Scavenger Hunt

What makes exploring the world even better? Exploring the world while hunting for random things. That's right, a scavenger hunt! Scavenger hunts are so much fun. They also happen to be great for bringing bickering friends together. One day, Cass and Eugene were in the middle of their thirty-seventh fight of the day (*not* an exaggeration, people), so I put together a scavenger hunt and forced them to play. They started out arguing as usual, but then they began to work together and ended up getting along and actually liking each other (well, almost).

GETTING STARTED

First, come up with a list of what you and your friends will have to find. It's best to make two lists: one for things to collect, and one for things to spot—since there are lots of things that really can't or shouldn't be collected.

READY, SET, SEARCH!
Once you've made your lists, decide if you are going to work as teams or by yourselves. Then make a list of the items for each player or team.

For the items you'll be collecting, decide if you want to pile them up in a certain spot or if you want each person (or each team) to have a bag or a box. For the items to spot, players can check them off their lists as they spot them and just jot down the location. When everyone is ready to start, begin the hunt.

Your lists might look something like this:

To Spot

1. Bird's nest
2. Frog
3. Butterfly
4. Tree stump
5. Grasshopper
6. Animal tracks
7. Wo rm
8. Stream
9. Squirrel
10. Moss

To Collect

1. Acorn
2. Pine needle
3. Yellow flower
4. Feather
5. Sparkly rock
6. Red leaf
7. Piece of bark longer than your finger
8. Flower petal
9. Seed
10. Bumpy stick

Scavenger hunts are fun in the village, too. My father always sends at least ten guards to escort me, but that doesn't stop me! I just convince them all to join in the hunting fun!

VILLAGE HUNT

To Spot
1. Fountain
2. Someone with a mustache
3. Bell
4. Clock
5. Someone laughing
6. Black boots
7. Baby
8. Book
9. Someone wearing a hat
10. Yellow sign

To Collect
1. Bread crumb
2. Napkin
3. Leaf
4. Piece of fruit
5. Toothpick
6. Newspaper
7. Piece of candy
8. Coin
9. Flower
10. Cupcake wrapper

Flower Crowns

I just adore creating crowns using fresh flowers! They're fun to make and pretty to wear. I'll admit, sometimes I go a little overboard when it comes to making these little flowery beauties. But I just can't seem to stop until everyone—even Pascal—has one!

First, collect flowers. Try to find flowers with long, flexible stems that bend a little to make weaving easier. Once you have enough flowers, start braiding the stems together.

Add more flowers as you continue to braid, weaving them in to create a long chain. Once your chain is long enough to fit around your head, fasten the ends together with another bunch of stems or a small piece of string.

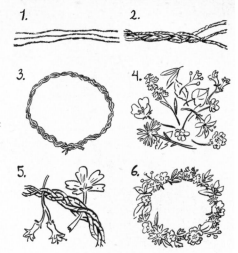

1.
2.
3.
4.
5.
6.

Card Games

'You know what 'I love about card games? 'You can play with just about anyone, anywhere, anytime. Whether it's rainy and cold and you're warm and toasty inside by the fire or it's a perfectly sunny day and you're out in a grassy meadow–you can break out a deck of cards and let the fun begin!

Setup

Deal out all the cards, one card at a time. Players should place their stacks of cards in front of them, facedown.

Play

Starting with the top card, each player should flip one card faceup and place it in the center. Whoever flipped over the higher of the two cards gets to keep those cards. Players should place their collected cards next to them in a separate pile. The object of the game is to collect more cards.

If both players flip over the same card, it's "war." To fight the war, each player puts three cards facedown and a fourth card faceup. Whoever has the higher faceup card gets all the cards.

If both players flip over the same

card again, it's another "war" and each player should put three cards facedown and a fourth faceup. Though its not very likely, "war" can continue this way multiple times until the players flip up different cards. The player with the higher value gets the whole pile.

The game ends when all the cards have been played. The player with the most cards is the winner.

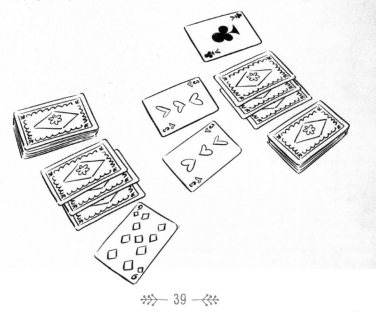

Setup

Slapjack is a game that can be played with as many players as you'd like. Deal out the cards equally among the players. Just like in War, players should put their stacks facedown in front of them.

Play

In this game, players try to collect cards by being the first to slap one of their hands on a jack. Each player takes a turn flipping a card faceup and placing it in the center. (No peeking! Looking at your card before you flip it over is no fun and no fair.) If you see a jack . . . slap it! But be careful. If you slap a card that's *not* a jack, you have to give away a card to each player as a penalty.

The first player to slap a jack gets the pile. And just like War, the winner is the person who collects the most cards.

Keep a close eye on those cards when playing this game, especially when you play with Pascal. When that little tongue of his flicks you, boy, does it hurt!

SETUP

In this game, you *do not* want to end up with the old stinky moldy cheese. Choose an extra card or a joker to be the old stinky moldy cheese. You can write on or decorate it, but make sure it still looks like any other card from the back. Shuffle the cards and deal them equally among the players.

PLAY

Players should look at their cards, but hold them so no one else can see them. If you happen to have the old stinky moldy cheese card, put on your best poker face.

Once everyone has their cards, players should look for pairs and put them aside, facedown.

Now, as the dealer, fan out your cards and hold them out to the player on your left. That player should be able to see only the backs of your cards. The player picks a card out of your hand. If it's a match to one of the cards the player is holding, it can be paired up and placed facedown with the player's other pairs. And if it's the old stinky moldy cheese card, that player had better put on a poker face!

Next, that player holds the cards out to the next player on the left, who picks one card. Play continues this way until the cards have all been paired off except for the old stinky moldy cheese. Whoever ends up with that dreaded card loses, and the person with the most pairs wins.

The Game of Chess

Chess is a great game to play with a friend. Pascal and I play it all the time. And once you have a board and the pieces, you can start a game anywhere–from a tower to a castle, even outside on some grass during a nice sunny day (that last one is my favorite).

$\mathcal{E}$ach player has the same number of pieces. Each piece has its own special way of moving across the board.

To set up the board, place it between you and your opponent so that you both have a light square on your bottom right side. Set the pieces on the board like this:

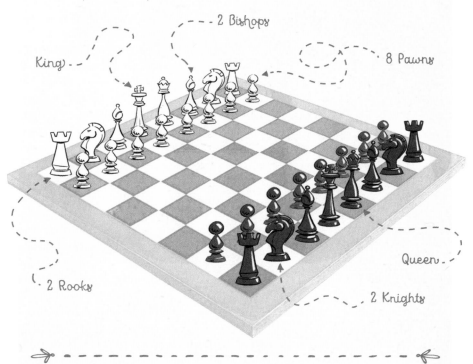

King

2 Bishops

8 Pawns

2 Rooks

Queen

2 Knights

PAWN

Your pawns are usually the first pieces to move. They typically move forward one space at a time, but on a pawn's very first move, you have the option of moving it two spaces ahead instead of one. Pawns move diagonally to capture.

Rook

Rooks move in a continuous line horizontally or vertically. They can go as far as you want them to in one turn (as long as there is not a piece blocking them), and they can move forward and backward. They can capture any piece in their path.

Bishop

The bishop is similar to the rook because it can move as far as you want it to as long as there are no pieces in its way. Like the rook, a bishop can capture any piece in its path.

Knight

Knights move in a special pattern, and as long as there is a spot for them to land in, they are able to hop over pieces in their path. They move in either direction in an L shape and capture opponent pieces they land on.

King

The king can move in any direction, but only one square at a time. It captures any piece that it lands on.

QUEEN

The queen can move diagonally, horizontally, forward, backward, and side to side. This piece can move one space at a time or continuously, like the rook and bishop. Any piece the queen lands on is captured. The queen is considered to be the strongest piece in the game.

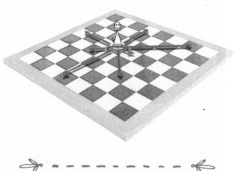

PLAY

White typically goes first. The object of the game is to capture your opponent's king. As you try to get closer to it, you capture other pieces in the way. Captured pieces get taken off the board. Think carefully about each move—you don't want to capture your opponent's pieces but put yourself in a dangerous position.

When you are in position to capture your opponent's king, say, "Check." If your opponent can move their king, play continues. But if their king is stuck, you say, "Checkmate." You have captured the king and won the game.

"My father likes playing chess every now and then. He will never admit it, but I think it bothers him that the king can't move across the board as easily as the queen. He likes reminding everyone that the game is all about catching the king. "That makes the king most important!" he always says.

Candle Making

Candles are so beautiful, aren't they? We have candles all over the castle. Their golden light just makes everything look warmer and cozier. Why not try making a candle? It's creative and fun, and it's the perfect sort of thing to do on a rainy day—or any kind of day, for that matter!

With an adult's help, put a pot of water on the stove to boil. While you're waiting, put the wax into the tin can.

Once the water is boiling, you can turn the burner off. Now carefully place the tin can into the hot water.

You can use a stick to gently stir the wax as it melts. Just be careful not to get any water in the wax.

Next, cut a piece of the wick and tie a small nut onto one end. The nut will act as a weight and help keep the wick straight as you dip it into the wax.

COLORFUL TWIST

Use old crayons to add a little color to your wax. (Be sure to peel the paper off first.)

Dip the wick into the wax a few times. Once you have a good amount of wax, hold it over the can to let it drip. When it stops dripping, hang the candle somewhere to dry. Wax dries fairly quickly, so you can even hold it until it's dry.

Remove the nut from the wick—the thin candle will be heavy enough to hang straight. Next, dip your candle in the wax again, let it drip over the can, and let it dry. Keep repeating this process until your candle is the thickness you like.

Okay, this candle didn't quite turn out the way I expected it to, but you know what? I think it's kind of great! If I turn my head to the side and squint my eyes a little, it sort of reminds me of Pascal doing a handstand in his sleep. Can you see it?

You can also make a candle inside a glass container. Cut your wick to the length you need, tie a nut to the bottom of the wick, and wrap the top of the wick around a pencil. Position the wick in the center of the container and lay the pencil across the top. Carefully pour the wax into the container. Once the wax dries, remove the pencil and trim the wick.

You can melt different-colored waxes to make patterns inside the container, too. Try layering the different colors to make stripes. Allow time to let the wax harden in between each stripe so that the hot wax doesn't melt into and mix with the previous color. Adding chunks of hard wax to the soft wax can also make an interesting design against the glass.

A simple way to add color is to use those old peeled crayon bits you probably have just lying around. They work great for a chunky or speckled look. Experiment with small pieces, shavings, or chunks of crayons.

Small dried flowers or petals along the glass can also look pretty. Just be sure you place the flowers close to the inside of the glass and not on top of the wick.

Saddling Up

Wouldn't it be fun to fly? Jumping into the saddle and riding Maximus is just about the closest I get to flying—well, that and using my hair like a rope to swing across a room. That feels a lot like flying, too.

Getting on a horse is called "mounting." To mount a horse, hold on to the reins and place one foot in the stirrup. Next, hoist your body up and swing your other leg up and over to the opposite side of the horse. Once you're sitting in the saddle, find your balance so that you feel safe, secure, and relaxed.

Your posture is important, because it helps you keep your balance as well as communicate with the horse. Try to keep your shoulders back and your chin up as you look ahead. Keep your feet in the stirrups and push your heels down a bit. Your legs should rest firmly against the horse's body.

Squeezing your legs tells the horse to go. So when you're ready, hold on to the reins with your hands and squeeze with your legs. Once you're riding, the way you sit is still very important, because it tells the horse how fast or slow you want to go. It's a sort of body language that the horse understands. When you lean forward, you're telling the horse to speed up, and when you lean back, you're sending a message to slow down.

Remember to stand to the side of the horse as you groom it. Standing behind a horse can make it nervous, and it may kick. It's always best to walk around the front of a horse when you want to get to its other side. If you do need to walk behind it, place your hand on its back and gently drag it along the horse's body as you slowly walk around.

This lets the horse know where you are, so it won't get nervous, startled, or confused to find you behind it.

A special pick is used to clear the dirt out of your horse's shoes.

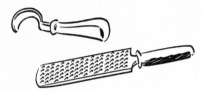

Grooming is fun for the horse *and* for the groomer (that's the person doing all the work). I still can't believe how many tools it takes to keep Maximus groomed. But he always looks so great, doesn't he?

After you pick out the dirt, use a brush to finish the job.

A currycomb is used to loosen up and lift the dirt off the horse before brushing it. It's like giving the horse a dry shower or bath as you move the currycomb in a circular motion across its coat.

Next, a regular stiff-bristled brush is used to brush away all the loosened dirt.

A softer-bristled brush is used next to make the horse's coat shiny. After that, use a small, very soft brush to carefully brush the horse's face around the nose and eyes. And finally, use a comb to get any tangles and knots out of the horse's tail.

How to Tell if a Horse Is in Love

I think Maximus definitely has a thing for Fidella. How can I tell? Based on the five signs that a horse is in love, that's how!

1 He looks straight ahead anytime the horse he loves walks by. Then he secretly watches her once she's passed.

2 He picks up his knees extra high as he trots by her—and holds his head extra high, too.

3 His *neigh* sounds more high-pitched whenever she is around.

4 He slows down whenever he walks by her stall. Sometimes he even pretends to have an itch just so he can stop and scratch it right in front of her!

5 He stares at her tail.

Self-Defense with a Frying Pan

Allow me to introduce you to my little friend, the frying pan. Don't let its size fool you. My frying pan is like a swift karate chop waiting to happen, and it's always there when I need it. There is no better way I know to defend myself against evildoers.

My frying pan has taken on dirty rotten thieves, evil wizards, and all sorts of other big meanies. Even Eugene and Cassandra can't help being impressed. So what guide would be complete without a few lessons in frying pan combat?

Cassandra insisted I make one thing absolutely clear: your frying pan combat skills should never be used on friends and family . . . unless, of course, they turn out to be evil wizards or dirty rotten thieves. But seriously, be careful. I'm telling you–the frying pan has unbelievable wrecking abilities. Only practice these moves when there is nobody else around!

This move is all
about the face of
the pan meeting the
face of your dirty
rotten meanie. Eye
the target as you
grip the frying pan
with both hands
and . . . *whack!*

For the Stir-Fry,
take your pan
and make tiny
up-and-down
movements with it
as you cover your
meanie with little
miniature hits.

Slide your feet while you grip the handle and make a big scooping move with your pan, as if drawing an imaginary U with it.

Eugene likes me to call this move "The Eugene-nado" since he invented it. Grab your frying pan and just start spinning around with it like a wild tornado!

Following Your Dreams

Everyone has dreams, but I think it takes a big giant dose of bravery to actually follow them. And nobody's better at following their dreams than my friends from the Snuggly Duckling, the pub thugs.

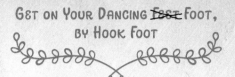

Get on Your Dancing ~~Feet~~ Foot, by Hook Foot

My dream was always to be a dancer, and I'm proud to say, you know what? I am! When I dance I feel like—I don't know—a happy bird or a wild streak of lightning across a dark night sky. And it's like every part of my body feels the music, and suddenly, everyone is watching me and wondering how my body can be so hypnotizing. It's like I put everyone under a spell with my rhythm and movement. Anyhow, I'd be happy to give you some pointers on how to be a dancer. Try to keep up with me.

First things first—always limber up a little before trying to break into a dance. I like to stretch out every part of my body. I pay special attention to my muscular legs and arms. I also twist my waist a little to help loosen the hips up.

Next thing you need to do is find some music that makes you want to move.

You'll know when you've found it because your hook foot will start tapping or your legs will just start moving around uncontrollably. Maybe your fingers wiggle a little bit or your neck sways back and forth. All I know is that your body hears the music, just like your ears. And it responds. You'll just feel it and know it's right. Now crank up that tune and let yourself loose. It's time to dance! Release your body to the music and move across the floor. If you have a natural talent like me, watch out, because your dancing will likely make you extremely popular. Suddenly, everyone will be watching you and wishing they could move like you!

Big Nose's Guide to Romance

What would life be without romance? I don't even want to know. The thought of it just makes me sad. In a nutshell, romance makes us notice and appreciate the true beauty that is all around us.

So how do you show someone you love them? I think the best way is to tell them how you feel. And the best way to do that is with poetry. It's even better than a tattoo. Really, it's the most romantic thing in the world. The toughest part about writing poetry is keeping the pages dry. It can be a real challenge. Once you pull yourself together, you need to find a thinking place. The first thing you gotta do is think about the person you love.

What do you love about your person? Maybe it's their eyes or maybe it's their nose. Imagine that, right? It could be their kindness, their strength . . . or even the way their stomach sounds when they're hungry. If you're anything like me, you probably love just about everything. It's so easy to fall in love.

Now, how does the person make you feel? Do you get the feeling of butterflies fluttering around in your stomach when you see them? Or maybe they make you feel like you could lift a huge boulder right up off the ground. Whatever those feelings are, just write them down. And you know what? There are no wrong answers.

Okay, last question: What does the person make you think of? A pretty, sweet-smelling flower covered in dewdrops? The moon hiding behind some mysterious fog? Or maybe a delicious pot of beef stew with just the right number of potato chunks.

Next is the really fun part. You get to lump all of those romantic things together to make a poem. It can rhyme, but it doesn't have to. And don't worry about making it long or short—just let the words pour out and see what happens.

Here are two poems I wrote for my true love just the other day. They're pretty different, but they really capture the romance and love I feel for my lady. There is no right way or wrong way to write a poem when you write from your heart. (Now, how's that for poetic?)

My Flower

You. My flower.
Me. Need a shower.

Song to My Sweet Lovebird

Tweet. Tweet. You are so sweet.
I love your eyes and I love your feet.
I love the way you eat turkey meat.
To me, you always look like a treat.
You make me feel so very neat.
Tweet. Tweet. You are my sweet.

That one gives me goose bumps every time I read it. You too, right? Words can be so powerful. I'm welling up again. Happy poetry writing, and remember—no matter what, stay romantic. Keep love alive!

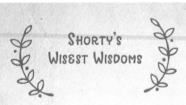

SHORTY'S WISEST WISDOMS

Well, since we're all sharing, I figure it's kind of my duty to hand over some of my best wisdom. It will surely improve your life.

→ If you can't stand on one foot, find a second.

→ When life makes you tired, give it a nap.
No, that's not right. I mean a slap. Give it a slap.

→ Cold noodles last more than a day.

→ Wake up in the morning and you're almost there.

→ If you think you're using a stick when you need a twig, you probably are.

→ Never take another man's whisker.

→ Just 'cause it's raining doesn't mean it ain't sunny somewhere.

→ Sometimes ya gotta take out the trash.

→ Stand where you are to find your gold . . .
or you could sit.

→ A fish in a dish is better than one in the face.
At least usually.

You're welcome.

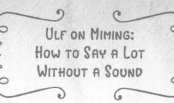

Shhhhh. Miming is acting something out without making a single sound. I'm not making a sound, but I'm using gestures to make you believe that there is a very high wall in front of me right now. It's so very high. It's so very thick. I can't climb over it. I can barely see over it.

It's like magic. I am making something appear out of thin air. Try it for yourself. I bet you'll love being a mime like me.

VLADIMIR'S UNICORN-COLLECTING TIPS

If you like unicorns like me, you should collect them. It's fun. I love unicorns.

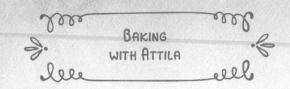

Well, hello, and welcome to my baking section. Baking is a way for me to show my happiness and share it with the people who like to eat my stuff.
Cupcakes are one of my favorite things to bake. And they are also one of my favorite things to eat. But I also really like cream puffs. And fudge.

ATTILA'S SWEET CAKES

This is one of my favorite recipes because it's simple, but you can jazz it up any way you like. If you want to make cupcakes, use a little cupcake pan (and liners if you want to be fancy—I like the pink ones). Or you can use a bigger pan and make a full-size cake if that's what you're into.

INGREDIENTS

* ⁕ 2 cups flour
* ⁕ A pinch of salt
* ⁕ 2 teaspoons baking powder
* ⁕ ½ cup butter or oil
* ⁕ 1 cup sugar
* ⁕ 2 eggs
* ⁕ 1 cup milk
* ⁕ 1 teaspoon vanilla extract

MIX AND BAKE

Preheat the oven—I usually set it at around 350 to 375 degrees. Mix everything together to make the batter. Then bake it for about 30 to 40 minutes. You'll know it's done when you can stick a toothpick in and it comes out clean.

Top off your cake with some powdered sugar, whipped cream, or icing. Sometimes I put colorful sprinkles or a cherry on top, too.

JAZZ IT UP

This is a basic cake recipe, so you can add all kinds of things to make it your own, like cocoa powder, chocolate chunks, or bananas. I experiment with plenty of things just to see how they taste. Try stuff that sounds good to you. I tried adding bacon once, and guess what? The guys loved it, and now they ask me to make my bacon cakes all the time!

Just like Attila, I like to cook and bake. I love how he suggests adding your own spin to his recipe. If you're daring, why not try adding a couple of different things to the recipe, like your favorite candy or little pieces of fresh fruit? And don't forget to give your recipe a creative name. I'm mixing up a batch of "Rapunzel's Red Berry Razzle Dazzle Cupcakes" as we speak!

Bully-Eye

Playing darts is such fun! It involves hurling pointy things at a target, so it's a lot like archery, only you don't need as much equipment or as much space to play. It's also not as dangerous . . . unless you happen to be playing with Eugene!

To play darts, you'll need a dartboard, some darts, and a place to hang the board. The object of darts is pretty straightforward—stand about seven feet from the board, take aim, and try to hit the target. You can play darts alone, with friends, and even in teams. Here are a couple of games to try:

CRICKET

Cricket is a dart game for two players. Create a scoreboard with the numbers 15 to 20 written up the middle. Then write a "B" on top, above the 20, for "bull's-eye." Write one player's name on one side of the scoreboard and the other player's name on the other. Each player gets three darts. The first player tries to hit one of the numbered triangles from 15 to 20, or the bull's-eye. The object of the game is to complete the scoreboard first. The first player to hit every number on the scoreboard and the bull's-eye, three times each, wins. Keep track of each hit with a slash mark.

You can earn three hits without hitting the number three times. Each number has different sections on the dartboard. Each section earns a different value. Take a look at the diagram. So if you hit the smallest inner part of the number 20 (3 on diagram) on your first throw, that counts as three and you have closed out that number. If you hit the smallest outer part (2) you get two hits, and the largest parts (1) count as one.

Go Solo

Playing darts on your own can be as simple as seeing how many throws it takes you to get a bull's-eye, but there are also a couple of games you can play.

"Around the Clock" is a solo game where you try to get every number on the board in order, saving the bull's-eye for last.

Cricket is another game you can play by yourself. Keep track of your score and see how long it takes you to hit all your targets. You can also create a cricket-type board for yourself using any numbers you like. Use your lucky numbers, or add two bull's-eyes to your list— meaning you'll need to hit six bull's-eyes in all!

Pottery

I think of clay as a cousin to mud, and you know how I feel about mud! Whether I'm just playing around or molding something beautiful, clay feels great in my hands. And there is something super satisfying about starting with this big shapeless lump and turning it into something unique.

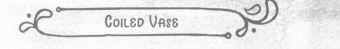

Coiled Vase

Step 1

Roll a small amount of clay out into a flat piece that's about a quarter inch thick and trim it to size with a dull knife. Think about how big you want your vase to be. This piece will be the bottom of it, so cut accordingly. (Clay can shrink a little once it dries, so it's a good idea to make the bottom a bit bigger than it seems like you should.)

Step 2

To create coils, roll a piece of clay between the palms of your hands or against a table. The coil should start to get longer as it stretches out and become thinner and thinner.

Each coil's length and thickness is up to you. The number of coils you make depends on the thickness of the coils and how big you want your vase to be. Remember, you can always make more coils if you don't have enough once you start building your vase.

Choose Your Shape

Your vase can be any shape you want, so don't feel like you have to make a circle. How about making a heart-shaped vase, or maybe one that's triangular or square? Try different things to find what *you* like.

Step 3

To begin building, place the first coil around the bottom of the vase. Curl the base up and around that first coil and use your fingers to blend them together. Once it is smooth, add another coil on top of the first.

Continue to build the vase using the coils until it's the height you want. Use your fingers to blend the coils into each other as you build, making sure they stick together. If your clay starts to feel dry or hard, just wet your fingers as you work.

If you want your vase to be straight, build up the coils evenly. If you prefer curves, try adding coils of different lengths.

Feel free to change as you go. If you decide you want to make the vase a little thinner, just take off a coil or two and wrap it tighter. Keep working with your clay until you figure out what you like.

Once you're happy with the shape of the vase, set it somewhere to dry and then paint it to finish it off.

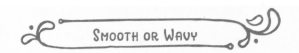

Smooth or Wavy

Do you like the smooth look, or do you like the wavy look of the coils? If you want your vase to look smooth, use your fingers to blend the outsides of the coils together as you go. But if you like the texture of the coils, just smooth the inside of your vase and leave the outside looking coiled.

Sometimes I like creating little spirals of clay and piecing them together to form my vase. See? The spirals and swirls give my vase a completely different look. I made about thirty of these pretty vases to hold the centerpieces at the royal banquet my father hosted last week. I have to say, the banquet was just as boring as the one before it, but I thought it was the most beautiful one yet—the vases were unique and made the tables look completely WOW!

"I made a small pinch pot, put a flower in it, and gave it to my mother as a gift—just to make her day a little brighter!

PINCH POT

Pinch pots are probably the simplest things you can build with clay. The basic technique involves forming a ball out of clay and then using your fingers to pinch or squeeze it into the shape of a pot. And just like you can with coiling, you can use this technique to make a lot of different things.

STEP 1

First, decide how big you want your pot to be. Then, take a piece of clay that is smaller than the size you want. Next, make a big ball with your clay. Roll it against the top of a table or between the palms of your hands until you have a nice smooth ball.

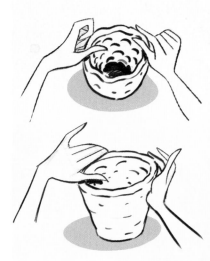

Step 2

Hold the ball of clay in one hand and push your thumb into its center to make a pit. Be sure to leave at least a quarter inch of clay at the bottom to hold the pot together.

Continue in this way, using your thumb and turning the ball as you push more and more to shape the pot. The first pit you made with your thumb will get bigger and bigger. As you turn the clay, pinch the outside walls of the pot with your fingers to try to make it even all the way around.

Adding Texture

You can add texture to clay by using a tool like a pencil, a toothpick, or even a piece of lace. One way to do this is to carefully carve a design into your clay object before it dries. Just use a sharp tool to carve wavy lines, stars, flowers, or even words into the clay.

You can also imprint the clay *before* molding your creation. Place a piece of lace on the clay and use a rolling pin to transfer the lacy pattern onto its surface. You can imprint other designs, too. Things like leaves, vines, or flowers can create interesting designs. Just remember to carefully remove them after you imprint your clay.

Sun Salutation

Stretching is just one of those things that helps me feel great. And really, with all this open space, I find myself doing it all the time. Inside the tower I could practically touch both walls at the same time, which made stretching just a little bit difficult. But out here, the possibilities are endless.

This sun salutation is a series of relaxing poses and stretches that also focuses on breathing. I greet just about every morning with a sun salutation. (Pascal likes it, too.) With the light streaming into my bedroom, it's the perfect way to say, "Good morning, sun!" Give it a try some morning . . . or at any time of day, for that matter!

Wear loose, comfortable clothing . . . and here's the really good news: when doing this type of stretching, going barefoot is encouraged!

1

Stand with your feet about hip width apart.

2

Inhale as you reach your hands up to the sky. Slightly arch your back and neck as you stretch up and reach back behind you a little bit.

4

With your hands on the floor, inhale as you lift your head to look up.

5

Exhale as you jump or move your legs back—but keep them straight. Use your arms to hold your body up and slowly lower your body to the floor (like a pushup).

3

Exhale as you bring your hands around and reach down to touch your toes.

6

Inhale as you press your hands against the floor and look up to the sky. This position is called "cobra," because the front part of your body rises up from the ground kind of like a cobra's.

I like to take lots of deep breaths—especially when things get a little hectic. And I have to say, "hectic" is a pretty good way to describe this whole royal thing.

7

Exhale as you use your arms and legs to push your body up. Keep your hands and feet on the floor and stretch out your back. You can rise up onto your toes to stretch them out, too.

8

Inhale as you bring your feet up to where your hands are and lift your head to look up.

10

Inhale as you rise up and reach to the sky again. Stretch up as you arch backward a bit.

11

Bring your arms down to rest as you exhale. You're back to where you started.

9

Exhale as you fold your head down to your knees and touch your toes or grab your legs.

12

The twelfth step is all about the mouth stretch. Open your mouth as wide as you can and stretch from ear to ear.

This position is called "downward dog." Have you ever seen a dog stretch after a nap? It looks a lot like this pose.

Making Knots

Tying knots is one of those skills that can come in super handy, and not just for those with hair long enough to swing from. But hey, you never know when you'll need to use your superior knot-tying skills—for anything from horseback riding and rock climbing to crafts and jewelry making. Every creative and brave person should know how to tie these basic knots!

Overhand Knot

Using one piece of rope, make a small loop by crossing the bottom over the top. Push the rope through the back of the loop and pull it tight.

Square Knot

You'll need two pieces of rope for this knot. First, take the right piece of rope and put it over the left. Tuck it under and lift both pieces up. The two pieces of rope look a little tangled together and have swapped places. Take the left piece of rope (which was originally the right piece), cross it over the other piece, and tuck it under and through the loop. Pull both pieces to make a square knot.

Figure-Eight Knot

For this knot, you'll need one piece of rope. First, take the end of the rope and make a loop. That loop is the bottom of the 8. Next, bring the end of the rope around the back of the straight part of the rope to make the top of the 8. Bring the end over and through the front of the bottom part of the 8, and you've tied a figure-eight knot.

Slipknot

Using one piece of rope, make one big loop. Cross the right side over the left to make the base of the loop. Bring the right side through the loop, but don't pull it all the way through. Hold the tail of the right side and the left while you pull the top of the right rope through the big original loop with your other hand to tighten the knot. If you pull both tails of the rope and the knot "slips" out, you tied it correctly.

String Games

Who would've ever thought that you could have so much fun with a simple piece of string? I played string games often when I lived in the tower, because I always had something I could use as string on hand–or maybe I should say "on head," as in my hair! But playing with a friend is so much more fun than playing alone. With just a little

bit of know-how and a piece of string, yarn, or rope (or unnaturally long hair), you can play games or even create string art. All you need is a piece of string or rope about twice as long as your arm. Tie the ends of the string together to make a big circle that won't come loose. (Put those knot skills to use!) Now you're ready to go!

1 Loop both sides of your string circle around your thumbs and pinky fingers and let it run across your palms.

2 Use your right pointer finger to grab the string on the left palm. To do this, put your pointer finger under the string across your left palm. Pull the string back toward your right side. Do the same thing with the left pointer finger.

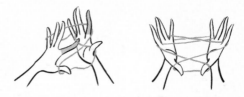

3 Drop the loops from your thumbs and reach across, under all the strings, to hook the farthest string with those thumbs. Pull the string back using both thumbs.

4 Use your thumbs again, this time to reach over the first string and under the second string. (Both the first and second strings should still be held by the pointer fingers.)

5 Drop the strings from your pinky fingers. Spread out your fingers.

6 Hook your pinky fingers over the string closest to them and under the next string.

7 Drop the loops from your thumbs and hold them up to your face to show off your cat's whiskers.

Cat's Whiskers is the simplest string art I know. I love the way the whiskers just pop up after I drop my thumbs in the last step.

CUP AND SAUCER

A lot of string art starts with the same first steps as Cat's Whiskers.

1 To make the cup and saucer, you start like the whiskers—place the string circle across your palms and around your pinky fingers and thumbs.

2 Reach across with your right pointer finger and grab the string going across your left palm. Pull it back to the right side and do the same with the left pointer finger.

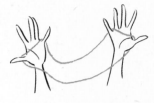

3 With your thumbs, reach over the first pointer-finger string, under the second pointer-finger string, and over the top string.

4 This move is a bit tricky, so take it slow. There should now be two loops around your thumbs. Slip your thumbs through the lower loop.

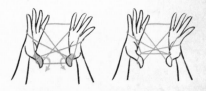

5 Drop the loops from your pinky fingers and tilt your thumbs up. Can you see the cup and saucer?

Cat's Cradle is a string game that can be played with two people and one string.

1 The first player sets up the string in the same way as before—loop both sides of the string around your thumbs and pinky fingers so it runs across your palms.

2 Take your right middle finger, hook it underneath the string going across the left palm, and pull it back. Do the same with your left middle finger to create the "cradle."

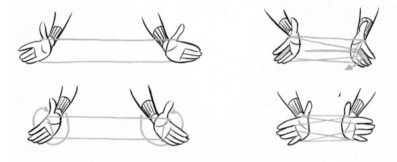

3 Now the other player goes. Look for the place where the string makes two Xs. Use your pointer fingers and thumbs to pinch those Xs. That's how to get the string from player one and place it on your own hands.

Pinching the Xs, take them over the outside strings and turn them up in between those strings. Stretch the pointer finger and thumb apart. Player two should now be holding the cradle.

4 This time, player one is looking for the two middle Xs. Pinch the middle Xs and bring them over and under the outside strings. Hopefully, player one has the string now and it looks kind of like candles.

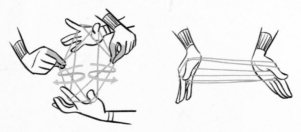

5 Player two, looking down on the candles, you're going to focus on the two in the middle. Grab the left side with your right pinky and the right side with your left pinky so the strings cross. See the triangles? While keeping the string hooked on your pinky fingers, dip your pointer finger and thumb down into those big outside triangles and push them up through the middle.

6 Now you can probably see the Xs again. Player one, pinch the Xs and pull them out. Push your fingers down through the middle and pull apart.

7 Player two, pinch the Xs with your pointer finger and thumb. Bring the Xs over the outside string and up through the middle.

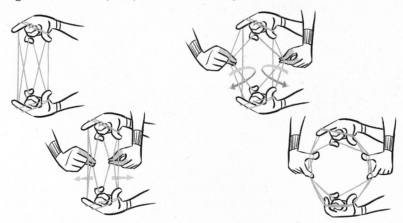

8 Now there should be a diamond in the middle with triangles around its edge. This is the cat's cradle! You can end the game here or keep playing by passing the string back and forth between you in the same way.

The Art of Folded Paper

With a few little folds and some creative flair, you can turn an ordinary square piece of paper into something amazing! Make it heartfelt and give it to someone you love, or make it magical, like the paper lanterns Eugene and I launched into the sky one night not so long ago. No matter where your creativity takes you, paper crafts are simply extraordinary.

1 Hold a square piece of paper like a diamond. Bring the top point to the bottom point and fold. Open the paper and bring the right point to the left point and fold. Open the paper. Now you have have two creases that meet in the center. These are guidelines.

2 Fold the top point of the diamond down so that the tip hits the center crease (1). Fold the bottom point up to the top of the top fold (2).

3 See the big triangle in the middle of the paper? Grab the lower right point of the triangle and fold it up to the top point of the triangle. Do the same on the left side.

4 Turn over. Fold the top two points down and the two side points in toward the center as shown to give the heart its curves.

5 Turn your paper heart over and decorate it however you like!

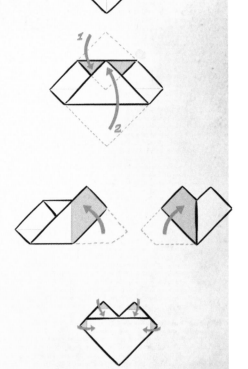

1 First make guidelines in your paper by folding in half four times (unfold paper after each fold): top corner to bottom corner, right corner to left corner, and edge to edge in both directions. Your paper should now have creases that look like the diagram below.

2 Position the paper so it looks like a diamond. Fold the top point and bottom point to the center crease as shown.

3 Flip the paper over. Fold the top edge down and align with the center crease. When folded, there should be a triangle sticking above the top edge of the shape. Repeat with the bottom edge. The two triangles should form a diamond shape.

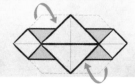

4 Fold the points of the top and bottom triangles to the center crease.

5 Take the left side of the paper and fold it so the point touches the right-most diamond shape as shown. Push down to crease. Do not unfold.

6 Fold the paper back to the left along an imaginary line 3/4 inch from the left edge. See the diagram below to make sure you've folded correctly.

7 Fold the top edge down to align with the center crease. Unfold. Do the same with the bottom edge. Unfold. Now fold down the two little corners of the left section of the sword as shown. Unfold.

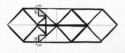

8 To make the sword handle, grab the top edge of the left section of the sword and gently bend down to the middle crease. This will create a small pocket. Flatten the pocket. Do the same with the bottom edge. Last, fold in the point on the left to create a straight edge to the handle.

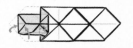

9 Take the left side of the handle and fold it to touch the right-most diamond shape. (**a**) Accordion-fold the handle back to the left. (**b**)

10 Fold up the bottom edge of the sword blade to align with the middle crease, tucking the end under the handle piece. Do the same with the top edge. Your sword is complete.

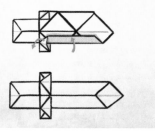

One of Cassandra's favorite things is her sword. She made a paper sword that looks a lot like the real one and gave it to me. She thought I should practice with the paper one before trying to use the real thing, which is probably a good idea.

1 Create two corner-to-corner creases in a square piece of paper as shown. Unfold.

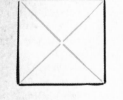

2 Take each corner and fold its point into the center.

3 Flip the paper over and fold each corner to the center.

4 Fold in half. The four paper flaps should be on the outside. Then fold in half again into a square. Unfold.

5 Put your pointer fingers and thumbs into the flaps. The fortune-teller should now open and close when you move your pointer fingers and thumbs together.

6 Decorate by drawing colors (or any other thing you choose) on the four outside flaps. Then unfold and write numbers on the inside triangles. Open the flaps and write a fortune underneath each one. Fortunes can be whatever you want them to be—adventurous, romantic, or even silly. Some examples are "You will soon go on a long journey" and "Your destiny is to find true love."

N ow that your fortune-teller is done, find a friend to play! Hold the fortune-teller out and ask your friend to select one of the four things you chose for the outside flaps.

Next, spell out the word of the color or picture your friend chose as you open and close the fortune-teller once for each letter.

Now have your friend choose one of the numbers that is showing on the inside. Count as you open and close the fortune-teller that many times. Have your friend choose one more number that is showing on an inside flap. Then lift the flap that has that number on it and read your friend's fortune.

Fortune-tellers are fun and can help to pass the time when you're super bored, like during royal summits that feel like they'll never end, or official ceremonies that go on and on . . . and ooooooon. Make one and use it to find your own fortune or figure out the fortunes of your friends!

These paper lanterns are quick and easy to make, so you can create a lot of them in no time at all. You can make them in different sizes, too.

1 If you'd like to decorate your lantern with paint, stamps, or colored pencils, do that first.

Cut a thin strip off a sheet of paper and set it aside for later. Next, fold the paper in half vertically left to right.

3 Unfold the paper. You should have rows of long slits cut into the paper now. Hold the paper so that it is vertical and tall. Curl it so that the ends meet to make a cylinder. Now tape or glue the ends together, both at the top and bottom.

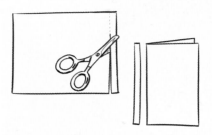

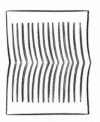

2 Now take the folded paper and cut lines across the fold—about three-quarters of the way to the end. You can choose to make these cuts even or uneven, but make sure you don't cut all the way through to the other side, or your lantern will fall apart.

4 To add a handle to your lantern, simply take the strip of paper you set aside and tape or glue it from one side of the top to the other.

Lanterns always make me smile. I can't look at one and not think about how they reunited me with my parents. That's why I have a bunch of them hanging from the ceiling of my bedroom. When I open my eyes every morning and see them there, I just feel happy! I made a bunch of mini lanterns and hung them on a piece of string across the dining hall. Of course, my father absolutely loved it, since lanterns remind him of being reunited with me, too!

Social Graces

I have to admit, getting used to living in the castle has definitely been a little bit of–okay, a *huge* adjustment for me. The fact that I'm a princess means I'm supposed to have good manners, know how to be polite, and be perfect at doing all those princess-y things, like bowing or curtsying at the right moment and eating with the correct fork. Oh, and let's not forget about always having to wear shoes! So I thought I'd include a little section on social graces, mostly because I think they can be really confusing.

Cassandra has lived in the castle forever, so she really knows how to do everything just right. I rely on her when it comes to everything proper, including curtsying. So apparently there are times for bowing, but then sometimes I'm supposed to curtsy. The curtsy is a little more involved, but let's see here . . . okay. When a curtsy is required, I'm usually wearing a dress or a skirt. I use both hands to pick up a tiny piece of the skirt or dress on either side. But not in the front, and not too high or too low. And while I lift the sides of the dress or skirt just a little bit, I'm supposed to lower my chest toward the ground. But wait! What if I'm not wearing a dress? It's not like I can lift up my pants . . . or can I? I'd better ask Cass about that one. Anyway, as I lift the sides of the dress or skirt and lower my chest toward the ground–gosh, this is a lot to remember–I'm simultaneously supposed to stretch one toe out to the side (which side, I have no idea) and smile and make eye contact with the person I'm curtsying to. Oh, and by the way, this should all be done gracefully (meaning without falling flat on my face).
Yeah, right.

It seems like most of the rules I'm supposed to follow begin with either the word *never* or the word *always*. So I've been taking notes, since you never know when you'll need to remember them.

Always chew with your
mouth closed.

Never slurp your soup.

Always try your best to
remember everyone's name.

Never put too much food in
your mouth at once.

Always welcome guests with
a smile and either a curtsy
or a bow (remind me to ask
Cassandra when to do which).

Never chew with your
mouth open.

Always show gratitude. Send a
thank-you note to show your
appreciation.

Never do anything to make
guests feel unwelcome.

Always wear shoes to parties
and special events.

When holding a teacup, you
should delicately wrap your
fingers around the handle to
lift it off its saucer. Quietly
sip (never slurp) and then
gently place it back down.
Try to make the least amount
of noise possible throughout
the entire ordeal. The same
goes for eating meals—
especially soup.

Treat Yourself

'While castle life has been a little tricky for me to adjust to at times, there is a certain someone who has managed to embrace the good life . . . with remarkable ease.

Life has changed quite a bit for me since moving into the castle. But I have to say, I've managed to adjust to it quite smoothly. It's been challenging at times, but honestly, I've now come to a point where I couldn't feel more at home here.

I've been primped, polished, and pampered with the best of them and have come out looking, well, even better! So I thought, why not share some of my pampering know-how with you so you can experience the good life, too?

You know what they say: When the going gets tough, the tough just smooth everything out with a good face scrub. Scrubbing your face is not only luxurious—it's a necessity. Keeping your skin looking excellent means you're always ready to flash a smolder.

Skin care should be fun, so why not play a little game to put your own recipe together. Pick one ingredient from each category to create your own customized facial scrub.

Smooth Stuff

* Honey
* Oil like olive oil/coconut oil/almond oil
* Yogurt
* Oatmeal
* Avocado
* Banana

Good-Smelling Stuff

* Vanilla extract
* Cinnamon
* Cocoa powder

Scrubby Stuff

* Sugar
* Brown sugar
* Salt
* Baking soda

Place your three ingredients in a bowl, mix it up, slather it on, relax, and enjoy. Rinse. Smolder. Repeat.

When I need a bit of extra pampering, I'll leave a scrub on my face for a little longer than normal to give myself a mask. Try it. It's incredible. Masks also work exceptionally well for frightening your friends. Bonus!

'Whether you live in a castle or a cottage, you can always find a way to experience the good life with a little "me time."

If you're anything like me, you're on your feet all day, running from hair appointments to spa treatments and so on. Yup. Life can be rough on your feet. So why not give them a treat? They deserve it. Fill a large bowl with warm water and place some big smooth stones or pebbles in the bottom for a little instant massage action. Oh, yeah . . . that's what I'm talking about.

Animal Encounters

The thing about the wilderness is . . . it's very . . . wild . . . and wilderness-y. And it's best if you know how to deal with all that wild-ness. Ever face, say . . . a bear? Me neither. But if you did, what would you do? Because if I did, I'm pretty sure I would throw my hands up in the air and just start screaming. Yes, that seems like the best thing to do at that particular moment.

Uh, no, not exactly, Fitzherbert. I think I'll take it from here.

So, yes, bears are one type of animal you might see in the wild. And no, you should not start screaming like Eugene on a bad hair day. A general rule with all wild-animal viewing is actually not to run and scream.

Loud noises, like screams and shrieks, can make wild animals think you are a threat and put them on the defensive. A defensive wild animal = not good.

Can you imagine sleeping for a whole month? Eugene told me he really wants to try it; he thinks it would be amazing for his skin. Well, grizzly bears do it every year when they hibernate. They sleep anywhere from four to seven months straight!

The best thing to do when you see a wild animal is to calmly watch from a safe distance and enjoy the view. It doesn't happen all that frequently—animals are very good at avoiding humans—so appreciate the moment.

If the animal does notice you, don't panic. Talk in a soft, quiet voice—it doesn't really matter what you say. You just want the animal to know you're a person and not an animal. So never try to imitate the sound of a wild animal. Just continue to talk quietly as you calmly walk in the opposite direction.

All sorts of creatures live in the forest. It's not always easy to spot animals in action, but you *can* find evidence that they've been there. From homes and structures that animals build, such as nests or tunnels, to things they leave behind, like a skunky smell or a snake skin, you can discover proof that an animal walked right in your path. Challenge yourself by finding the evidence and then trying to figure out what kind of animal left it. When you spot animal tracks, ask yourself questions to try to figure out what animal made them.

* What is the size of the track?
* How many toes does it have?
* Does it look like the animal has claws?
* Is there any webbing between the toes?
* Look closely—did the animal leave any hair or feathers behind?

Like a detective, you can use the answers to questions like these to figure out what type of animal made the tracks. You may even find more than just footprints. Some animals leave claw or bite marks in the places where they've searched for food. Keep your eyes open—you'll be amazed by what you discover!

Tracks aren't the only type of evidence animals leave behind. Snakes and lizards shed their skin as they grow, so you might find pieces of skin lying around the forest floor. Sometimes you can even find a complete covering of skin, from head to tail!

Reptiles are generally very quiet and quick, so if you encounter them in the wild, it will usually be for a very short moment.

One type of snake is not so quiet if you get close to it: the rattlesnake. If there are rattlesnakes in your area, listen for that telltale rattling noise. Stop moving immediately and look around to see where the snake is. Remember, these snakes shake the rattle to sound an alarm and send a message: *I'm here, and I don't want you to get any closer.* They really just want you to stay away. Once you locate the rattlesnake, back away slowly.

Most important, don't ever approach a rattlesnake or try to touch it. They can strike quickly, and their bites are venomous. If you do get bitten, do not try to suck the venom out. That will actually make it worse. Just stay as calm as possible, call for help, and wash the bite with soap and water if you can.

LOOK FOR THE LITTLE GUYS

It can be tricky to observe big animals in the forest, but don't forget about the little guys! Insects and other bugs are fascinating to watch, and you can always find them—as long as you know where to look. Just lift up a rotten log or a rock and uncover a bustling world. If you have a magnifying glass, use it to get an even closer look at the little critters. Remember to gently return the log or rock to its place after you're done observing so the bugs can get back to their normal activities.

A basic rule to follow: never try to draw a wild animal to your area with food. In fact, be sure to pack away all food, wrappers, and containers both before and after your snack or meal. Many animals are drawn to scraps, and you don't want to encourage them to come into your space. It's best to view wild animals in their natural environment, and that means viewing them from afar . . . not when they're rifling through your picnic basket or eating your snacks!

Mountain lions make loud purring noises and don't really roar. Have you ever heard one? It's kind of like what my father sounds like when he's snoring!

Outdoor Shelters

Every adventurer should know how to build an outdoor shelter. One time, Cass and I decided to hike to the falls, but before we could make it there, it started to rain. So we stopped and whipped up a shelter in a snap. Safe inside, we stayed nice and dry waiting for the storm to pass. We also scored a front-row seat to a massive rainbow afterward! But you don't always need a reason—you can build a shelter just for the joy of it. They're fun to build, and afterward, you have your own special spot to play games, tell stories, or just enjoy hanging out inside your creation.

LOCATION, LOCATION, LOCATION

Before building a shelter, search around for a good spot. The most important thing is having dry ground to build on. You don't want your shelter on top of mud or wet leaves. You also don't want to build too close to a lake, stream, or other water source. Just in case it does start to rain, you don't want the risk of water rising and getting to your shelter.

Another important thing is finding an area with level ground. It's more difficult and less sturdy to build on a sloped surface.

To build a tepee, find a sturdy tree on dry and level ground. Next, collect a lot of branches. If you have friends with you, it's a good idea to split the duties. Once you have enough branches to start building, have one group start to build while the others continue to collect more branches.

Lean the branches against the tree to form a tepee shape, crisscrossing them at the top. You can put them pretty close to each other as long as you leave a little space for a doorway. If you have rope or string, tie the top together for some extra security.

Once you have all your branches in place, cover them with some leaves or smaller, thinner branches.

This shelter is like a tent without a tarp. It's also called an "A-frame," because it looks like a giant A. To build an "A-frame" shelter, you'll need some rope and branches. The number of branches depends on how big you want it to be.

You'll need to find one extra-long branch for the top of the shelter. The others should be about half as long as the longest one.

"Cozy"? Not the exact word I'd use to describe this shelter. So, if it's all the same, I think I'll just hang out in the castle, where it's warm and *actually* cozy, and I'll see you tomorrow after my facial.

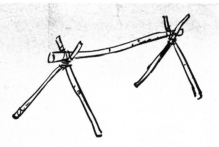

Start with two shorter branches and lean them against each other to form the letter A. Put the extra-long branch onto the peak of your A and tie the three branches together. Continue putting additional short branches in an A shape behind the first branches and underneath the long branch on top until your shelter is complete. For additional protection, cover your A-frame with smaller twigs or lighter leafy branches.

Extra Cozy

For a simple shelter that offers a bit more coverage, bring a tarp or blanket and a rope along with you. Simply find two trees to string the piece of rope between. The rope will be the top of your tent, so don't tie it too high or too low around the trunks of the trees. Throw the tarp or blanket over the rope so that the sides of the tarp hang over the rope evenly.

Place a few heavy rocks along the bottom edges of the tarp or blanket to hold the sides in place.

Climbing Trees

Climbing trees has to be one of my all-time favorite things to do. What could be more fun? Sometimes I see a tree and it just calls to me: "Climb me! See how high you can get." If there's a tree, I'm climbing it. And you know what I say? Leave your shoes at the trunk! Just like Pascal's, your feet and toes can help you climb any tree you see.

TREE-CLIMBING TIPS

✳ Find a tree with a strong trunk and thick branches, and be sure it can hold your weight.

✳ Use your hands and feet to steady yourself. Don't take a single step until you feel balanced and steady.

✳ Look up! Keep your eyes focused on where you're going, not where you've been.

✳ Be sure to check out each branch before you step onto it. Make sure you're choosing strong branches as you climb.

✳ Don't worry about reaching the very top. Just go as high as you're comfortable with.

✳ When you're ready to get your feet back on solid ground, go slow and steady all the way down.

PULL-UP

Design a pulley to easily bring things up into the tree. All you need is a long piece of rope and a bucket or pail with a handle. Throw the rope over a high branch of your tree and then adjust it so that both ends of the rope hang down evenly. Wrap one end of the rope around a branch to keep it in place and securely tie the other end around the handle of the pail. Now, when you've climbed up your tree and gotten settled, pull the pail up to get your stuff. Find a spot in the tree to rest the pail, and when you're ready to climb down, place your stuff back in the pail and slowly lower it down to the ground.

Pascal and I use pulleys all the time—it's the best way for him to get in and out of bed!

Fencing
with Cassandra

Fencing is a lot like dancing, and when it comes to dancing . . . well, let's just say I'm still learning–and stepping on a lot of toes along the way! But Cassandra has been fencing since she was a little girl, so it's no wonder she looks so graceful when she fences.

CASSANDRA ON FENCING

Y ou're right, Raps. Fencing *is* a lot like dancing. You have to be strong and graceful, and you need to have great balance and confidence in your steps. You also need to think fast and be willing to put in a lot of practice time. Remember that paper sword? Perfect for practicing anytime, anywhere. I enjoy fencing, and I think everyone should give it a whirl.

Equipment

Before you start, you'll need some equipment. A foil is a fencing sword. They are very lightweight and flexible, and they have blunt tips. You'll also need protective clothing, a mask, and . . . someone to fence against. If you are unable to find an opponent right away, you can get some targets and practice on them.

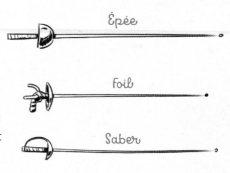

Épée

Foil

Saber

Grip your foil with your hand and rest your thumb against the guard. The guard is the piece that is between the handle and the blade.

Your pointer finger and thumb should be the focus of your grip. Be sure that your whole hand is beneath the guard—none of your fingers should be over the guard.

When two people are about to fence, a French term is spoken: *en garde*. It translates to "on your guard" and basically means "get ready." Both fencers get into position and the match begins.

A lunge is one of the most basic fencing moves. It's a move that says "attack." This is when you lunge at your opponent to strike with a stab or a slash.

To lunge, you keep your back leg straight while you bend your front leg and step toward your opponent.

The opposite of the lunge is called a "parry." This is a defensive move where you use your foil to defend yourself against your lunging opponent's foil. The goal here is to swipe your opponent's slash or stab out of the way before it hits you. Points are scored when you hit your opponent's chest with the tip of the foil. Typically, it's only a hit to the chest that counts when fencing with a foil.

En Garde

A foil is one type of sword used in fencing, but there are two other popular swords that are used. An épée is heavier than a foil and has a less flexible blade. A saber is similar in size to a foil but is wider and flat and has the most flexible blade of all.

The type of sword you use also has an impact on the rules of swordplay. With an épée, fencers can score points by hitting any part of the body with the tip of the sword. With saber swordplay, the upper body is the target, and fencers can hit that target with either the tip of the sword or the sword edge to score points.

Lunge

Parry

But some people will play with different targets. For example, you can decide that shoulders count, too. Feel free to decide where the targets will be, but to be fair, be sure you and your opponent decide together before you fence.

You can play to fifteen points to determine a winner or play three rounds that last a few minutes each. This is also something you should determine with your opponent before you begin.

Let's Experiment

Meet Varian. He's kind of like a mad scientist. He's good at taking regular old things, experimenting with them, and mysteriously turning them into something amazing! Varian calls what he does "alchemy," but I kind of think it's more like magic!

CRYSTAL GARDEN

Have you ever seen a crystal? They're pretty spectacular. You can actually grow your own crystals and make a crystal garden. There are all sorts of ways to make crystals, but here's one that is fairly simple:

First, cut up a sponge and place the pieces in a shallow dish or pan. You can make the sponge pieces any size you like.

Ask an adult to help you mix together one cup of boiling water with a quarter cup of regular old table salt and one tablespoon of vinegar. Stir the salt until it dissolves completely. You can add more salt if you like, but make sure it continues to completely dissolve into the water. (The salt is what will make the crystals.)

Pour the mixture into the shallow pan over the sponges. If you'd like your crystal garden to be colorful, drip some food coloring drops onto the sponges. It's fun to add different colors onto the different pieces of sponge.

Leave the dish somewhere where it won't be disturbed. Check it every day and prepare to be amazed as your crystal garden grows and grows. If you have a magnifying glass, use it to get an even closer look at the crystals.

Remember how the salt made the crystals form in that last experiment? You can actually make crystals that are deliciously sweet by using sugar instead of salt. You'll need to ask an adult to help with this one. Bring a cup of water to a boil and slowly add about three cups of sugar, half a cup at a time. Stir as you pour in the sugar to make sure it dissolves completely. Take the solution off the stove and add some dye or food coloring if you want a splash of color. Set it aside for a moment.

Next, find a clear glass jar that you can use to make your sugar crystals. Cut a piece of string a little taller than the jar. Tie the string around a pencil so that you can lay the pencil across the top and the string will hang down into the jar. (You don't want the string to touch the bottom of the jar, though.)

Dip the string into the sugar-and-water solution a few times to saturate it. Then remove it for a bit and let it dry. Pour the solution into the jar. Lay the pencil across the mouth of the jar and let the string with the dried solution on it hang down. You'll want the string to be at least a half inch from the bottom of the jar, but in the center of the liquid.

Find a place where you can leave your experiment for a few weeks without anyone disturbing it or moving it. Check it every day and watch as the crystals form. This experiment requires some patience, but the results are pretty amazing . . . and tasty, too!

When you are happy with the amount of crystals that have formed on the string, take it out of the jar and hang it somewhere to let it dry and harden. Once it's completely hardened, have fun eating your homegrown crystal treat!

Here's a little tip: Unless you're okay with sharing (er, giving away) your crystal treat, be sure to make more than one. Or hang your crystal candy somewhere, say, a former thief with a sweet tooth will not be able to find it.

Nighttime Games

What can you think of that's more fun than playing a game? Playing a game with a whole bunch of friends! And you know what makes games with friends even more exciting? Playing them in the dark! Whether you're inside or outside, the next time you have a group of friends gathered together, bring on your brave side. Turn out all the lights and play a nighttime game!

Sardines is a reversed version of hide-and-go-seek. First, choose a person to be it. In this game, everyone else closes their eyes and counts to fifty together as the one who's it hides.

Once the counting is over, players separate and everyone is on their own as they search for "it." The idea here is to be really quiet, because when someone finds "it," that player quietly squeezes into the hiding space.

The rest of the group continues to search for "it" and whoever else has joined the hiding space, hiding with them when they do. Before long, almost everybody will be squished into the hiding space like sardines. The last person to find the hiding spot is it for the next round.

Firefly Tag

You'll need a group of friends and a lantern to play this outdoor nighttime game. First, choose a place that you can call "home." It can be a tree, a boulder, or any specific spot that people can tag with their hands. Next, decide who is going to be it. The person who is it holds the lantern. If you're it, go to home and close your eyes as you count to fifty.

While you count, the other players hide. When you get to fifty, start searching for everyone. Anyone you shine your lantern on is caught. But you have to be able to see whomever you capture well enough to call out that person's name. Now that person joins you and begins to help search for the other players.

As you continue to search, anyone on your team can chase after other players you spot and tag them. If they get tagged, they join the it team. But a player who makes it to home without getting tagged or spotted is safe.

The game continues until everyone has been found or made it to home. The last person to be found or tagged is the winner and gets to choose who will be it in the next round. That person can choose to be it or choose someone else.

This game can be played outside in the dark, but we played once at night inside the castle with all the lights out, and it was fun and spooky at the same time! Pascal and I could never have played a game like this in the tower, just the two of us. Now that I have a whole group of friends to play with, there are so many new ways to have fun!

Rapunzel's Relays

Relay races are basically big group games that you can play outside in any open space. It's fun to split up and play in teams. Each player is counted on to get through the relay, so it's really important to work together as a team. Hmmm . . . now that I'm thinking about it, you know what? Relay races could be another way to trick Eugene and Cassandra into getting along!

WATER WAR

To have a water war, fill two buckets with water and place one in front of each team. Each team should form a line. Place an empty bucket behind the last player in line on each team. Then give each player a cup.

Someone should be designated as the referee. Once everyone is ready, the referee shouts, "Go!" If you're the first player, dip your cup into the water bucket and, without looking, tip the cup up behind you (over your shoulder or head) while the player behind you tries to catch the water. This continues down

the line until the last player dumps the water into the empty bucket.

While the water is making its way down the line, the front player continues to dip the cup in the water bucket and pass more and more water back until the bucket is empty.

You can either time this race and end it after a certain amount of time, or you can keep it going until the water buckets at the front of the lines are both empty. The winner of the water war is the team that has the most water in the bucket at the end of the line.

For this race, you each need a partner and a piece of rope. Before the race begins, tie your left leg to your partner's right leg. The object is to quickly walk or run to the halfway line and back with your legs connected. You really have to be coordinated and work with your partner to get those three legs moving fast. When you make it back to the starting point, tag the next three-legged pair of players on your team and watch them go.

The three-legged race is so much fun, it doesn't matter if you win, lose, or wind up falling flat on your face. If you're anything like me, you'll laugh until you cry!

For this relay race, you'll need pillowcases or potato sacks. Give one to the first player on each team. Decide where the halfway line is. It can be a tree, a big rock, or a piece of rope or string that you lay on the ground. The first racers for each team should put both feet into their pillowcases or sacks, holding them in place with both hands. When the referee shouts, "Go!" players begin to hop all the way to the halfway line, then turn around and hop back. As soon as they get back to the starting line, they have to get out of the sacks or pillowcases and give them to the next players on their teams. The race continues like this until everyone on the team has hopped to the halfway line and back. The first team to have all players complete the race wins.

If you trip or slip, it's okay. Just get up, adjust your sack, and keep going.

Obstacle Course

Use a variety of items, like hoops, balls, balance beams, and cones, to set up the obstacle course. Feel free to include relays as well. For example, you could include some spoons and eggs at one of the obstacle's "stations." Players would have to carry the egg on the spoon and make it across a finish line before moving on to the next activity in the course. You can also include some of the relay races described before.

Once you set up the obstacle course, form teams or agree to run through it individually. When it's time to go, see which team or individual can get through the course the fastest.

Building a Raft

There's really nothing like being on the water, but being on the water on a homemade raft makes it extra adventurous. So far, my friends and I have taken our homemade creations out on the lake behind the castle and the pond next to the village. No matter where you launch your raft, it feels amazing to build something that actually floats!

To make a raft, you will need some rope, twine, or strong vines. You'll also need a bunch of long logs or thick branches.

Collect a bunch of thick branches or logs that are about the same size and length to form the main part of the raft—or the "pad." Test the branches in shallow water before working with them to make sure they float. Once you have enough to make the pad of the raft, you will also need about half as many additional branches that are a bit longer than the ones you're going to use for the pad. These will help frame the raft.

1 When you have all your materials, you're ready to start building. To make the pad, lay out the shorter branches side by side on the shore near the water. Keep laying out branches until your pad is as big as you want it to be.

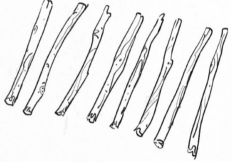

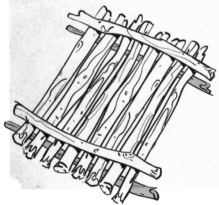

3 Next, place half of the longer branches underneath the shorter branches so that they're going in the opposite direction of the pad. Spread them out evenly and make sure they are straight.

3 Then place the other half directly above those, on top of the pad. Be sure that they line up with the long branches underneath and are also straight and evenly distributed. You're basically making a clamp to hold the branches together.

4 Now use the vines or rope to tie the ends of the framing branches together, squeezing the shorter branches between them. Tie them securely, crisscrossing and wrapping them around to fasten the branches.

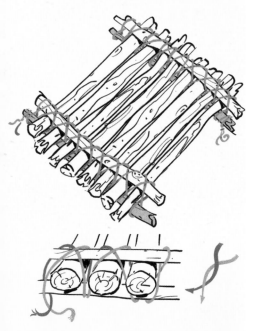

Try using one or more of the knots you learned about on page 81 to fasten the branches securely.

Once you've built your raft, try it out in calm, shallow water first . . . just in case it doesn't turn out as strong as you had hoped. Let's just say that the first few times I tried to make a raft, I ended up getting extremely wet!

Twig Boats

Aren't these tiny twig boats the cutest little things? The perfect thing about them is you can launch them anywhere–a lake, a stream, or even a large rain puddle.

You'll need twigs, sticks, and twine, string, or vines. You may also want to add a leaf for a sail and flowers for decoration.

Once you have your supplies together, take the twigs and sticks and tie them together in raft formation, the same way you did with the large raft. Use the twine, string, or vines to tie the longer framing sticks to the smaller sticks or twigs that make up the pad.

If you like, find a twig and a leaf to use for the mast and sail. Poke your twig through the bottom of the leaf and then back up through the top of it. Secure the twig to your little boat and you're done.

If you want to decorate your boat, add little flowers, pods, or seeds.

See how many things you can balance on your boat and still get it to float. Once I made a twig boat that was strong enough to hold Pascal!

Gone Fishing

I have to admit, I haven't actually caught many fish since trying my hand at the old rod and reel. But you know what? I don't really care! Sitting by the water with my fishing rod, just waiting to see if I'll get a bite, is half the fun!

Before going fishing, you'll need a fishing rod, some bait, and a place to store any fish you might catch, like a pail or a bucket.

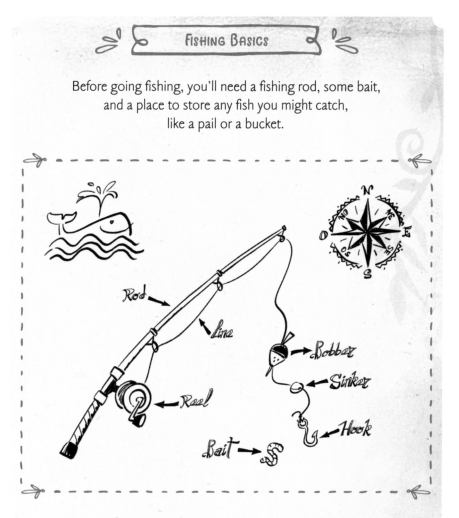

The *fishing rod* is a long pole with small loops on it to keep the fishing line in place. At the base of the rod is a reel. The *reel* is a giant spool of fishing line with a handle. The handle makes it easy to pull in the line after you've caught a fish (or when you just want to pull it in and try again).

A bobber, hook, and sinker are tied to the line. The *bobber* is a little float that bobs up and down in the water. When it bobs up and down, you'll know that a fish is nibbling on your bait. The *sinker* is a small weight that helps the bait and hook sink into the water. The *hook* at the very end of your line is where you attach the *bait* and how you catch your fish.

Baiting Your Hook

The hook is extremely sharp, so handle it with care. At first, it's best to ask someone who's baited a hook before to show you how. When you're not using the rod, keep the hook safely secured so that you don't poke yourself or anyone else with it.

Bait is what you use to draw the fish to your hook. Worms, crickets, and slugs all make good bait. Some people dig up worms called "night crawlers" at night and use them for bait. You can also catch small baitfish with a net.

Casting and Waiting

Casting means throwing your line into the water. When you're ready to cast, check to make sure no one is behind you. Then hook your finger around the line above the reel.

With one hand holding the handle and the other hand around the pole above the reel, carefully tilt the rod behind you over your shoulder. Next, fling the rod and line forward as you release your finger to let the line go. The weight of the sinker should carry the line out into the distance and then sink the hook into the water. Now you wait. . . .

Be patient as you quietly wait with your line in the water. If your bobber moves or if you feel a little tug on your line, start reeling the fish in. Then carefully take it off the hook. Decide if you want to throw it back and try again, or keep it to cook. But always be sure that any fish you decide to keep are safe to eat.

Chum

Chumming is another tactic used to draw fish. Mix up a bunch of different treats like meat, worms, and small baitfish (sardines work great) and crush everything into small bits. Before you throw your line into the water, throw some of the chum in. As soon as the fish catch sight of it, they usually swim right over to where you're fishing.

Night Fishing

Try night fishing and take a lantern to light up the water. Secure the lantern to the side of the boat—the light shining out over the water can help attract fish.

Most fish aren't that picky, so be creative! I've tried putting all kinds of things on my hook just to see what works—a slice of bacon, a piece of cheese, and even an anchovy. Pee-yew!

MAKE YOUR OWN

You can make a simple fishing rod using a sturdy stick, some string, fishing line, and a hook.

First, find a stick that is one or two inches and two to three feet long. Next, wrap the string around the top of the branch and tie it in place. Tie a long piece of fishing line on to the string and then thread the hook through the end of the line.

If you'd like to add a bobber to your fishing rod, use a cork. Just tie it on to the line about two feet above the

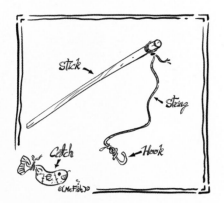

hook. For a weight, use a nut, metal beads, or anything heavy enough that you can easily tie on to the line a few of inches above the hook.

I don't know anyone who has caught more fish than Owl. I've been observing his fishing style, and here's what I've learned:

OWL'S FISHING TIPS

* Be quiet and patient . . . and wait.
* Give one area a good long try, but if you don't get any bites, move to another part of the water.
* Try fishing during different times of the day, like early morning just as the sun rises or late at night. This makes fishing a totally different experience.
* Be respectful of others fishing nearby.
* If you keep it, eat it.

The King's Safety Tips for Life

My dad takes safety veeeeeeery seriously. He always says, "A satisfying life requires great security." To him, it's one of the most important things—which is probably one of the reasons my dad and Maximus get along so well.

1. Remain aware of your surroundings at all times.
2. When exploring, bring a map, a compass, and a friend. Never explore new territory alone.
3. Mind signs and warnings—if it says "Keep Out," keep out.
4. If you need to call for help, do not hesitate.
5. Let your parents or guardians know where you are and where you will be.
6. Alert your parents or guardians if you are going to be late.
7. Surround yourself with people you trust.
8. Trust your instincts. If a situation feels unsafe, exit promptly.
9. When a problem arises, face it right away. Do not put it off.
10. Seek advice from your parents or guardians in any difficult situation.

Scary Tales

Great scary stories get my heart beating so loudly that I think everyone around me can hear it! To me, the best thing about scary stories is that they actually make me feel brave. Some of my favorite moments have involved sharing scary tales around a campfire with my friends. Between the quiet, the darkness, the moonlight, and the crackle of the fire, it's the perfect setting for a spooky story!

WHAT SCARES YOU?

One of the best ways to come up with an idea for a scary story is to think about what scares YOU. What are your greatest fears? What gives you goose bumps? Have you ever had a scary dream that still sends chills down your spine every time you remember it? Use it as a starting point to come up with a great scary tale to share.

SCARY TOPICS

Sometimes you need a little help making up a scary story. So here's a list of spooky topics to help get your stories going.

* A giant three-headed beast
* A cold and stormy night
* Creatures from the swamp
* A graveyard
* An old, creaky rocking chair
* An ancient, evil spell
* A mysterious key
* A 500-year-old cat
* An ancient underground city
* Black rocks that multiply and follow you

Play a story game with friends by choosing a story starter. Then take turns adding sentences or groups of sentences to build the story. Pass around an object like a stone or a feather to signify whose turn it is. A lantern is perfect if you're playing in the dark, and it makes the story even scarier. The person holding the lantern starts the story, and when they pass the lantern to the next person, that person continues. Pass the lantern around until the story is complete.

PERSPECTIVE

One spine-tingling technique is to tell the story from your own perspective. Start your tale by saying something like, "I've never told you this before, because it was too scary to repeat. But I think it's finally time I explained what happened to me one night a few years ago." Then tell the entire story using "me" and "I." Telling it from your own perspective makes it seem more real, and it will help your audience really get into your story.

Try using these story starters to help kick-start your tale.

* One night, a girl discovered a dark cave. She
  crept inside and was surprised to find . . .

* There once was a giant pine tree. On nights
  when the moon was full, its roots stretched out,
  far beyond the forest, and . . .

* A man couldn't sleep one night because a dog
  was howling and wouldn't stop. Finally, he went
  outside to find it and was shocked when he
  discovered that the sound wasn't coming from a
  dog at all. . . .

* No one ever went into the north part of the
  forest after dark, because . . .

* On his travels, a sailor came upon a deserted
  island and believed he had discovered it. But
  he soon found out that it was already inhabited
  by a group of strange creatures. . . .

* Two friends went hiking and eventually found
  themselves on top of a mountain where the
  fog was so thick they couldn't even see each
  other. Suddenly, they felt something brush by
  them. . . .

* A young girl stayed overnight at her
  grandparents' house. She was just about to fall
  asleep when she heard a strange noise. The
  sound led her to an old wooden box with a
  metal latch. She opened the latch, and . . .

Campfire Games

When my friends and I aren't roasting marshmallows or telling spooky tales around a campfire, we're playing games. Oh, and by the way, you don't need a campfire to play these games—you can play them anywhere, anytime. So gather your friends and get ready for some good old fun and games!

This game is great for a large group—the more players you have, the more challenging and fun the game will be. To start, everyone should sit in a circle.

One person (somebody who is not playing the game) picks the player with the poison ring. To start, all players should put their heads down and close their eyes. No peeking! Have the nonplayer walk around the edge of the circle and secretly tap one player on the shoulder. This player is the one with the poison ring. As play begins, everyone looks around at each other. The person with the poison ring should subtly wink at another player who is looking them in the eye at that moment. The wink means that person has been "poisoned."

The poisoned player silently counts to ten and then dramatically

pretends to have been poisoned. This can involve pretend choking, coughing, and plenty of dramatic facial expressions. Have fun with it and be as over the top as you want. For the finale, the poisoned player lies back, "dead," and is now out of the game.

Play continues as the person with the poison ring continues to wink at and poison other players.

If you haven't been poisoned yet and believe you know who the person with the poison ring is, say, "I have a suspect." If you guess correctly, you win the game. But if you get it wrong, you're out and should lie back, too.

If the player with the poison ring poisons everyone without getting caught, that player wins the game!

- -

EVERYONE WANTS TO PLAY?

If everybody wants to play, choose the one with the poison ring this way: Collect as many playing cards as you have players so that each person will get one. Make sure one of the cards is the deciding card and let everyone know which one it is. (The joker is a good choice—or even the old stinky moldy cheese card—just make sure there is only one type of that card in the deck.) Shuffle the cards and deal them out, facedown. Let everyone secretly take a peek at their cards. Whoever gets the deciding card gets the poison ring.

To start, one player sits in the "straight-faced seat" (just a designated spot for one player to sit). Another player sits in the "jokester seat." The object of the game is for the jokester to make the person in the straight-faced seat laugh. Here are the rules:

If you're in the straight-faced seat, you cannot close your eyes or cover your ears. If you show your teeth, smile, giggle, or laugh, it's counted as laughter and that round is over.

The jokester can do anything except touch the straight-faced player.

When everyone is ready, start the timer and see how long it takes each jokester to make the straight-faced player laugh. Once the player in the straight-faced seat smiles or laughs, stop the timer. Keep track of the timing for each player and see who makes everyone laugh the quickest and who can keep a straight face the longest.

Cassandra is the best at keeping a straight face. No one can beat her!

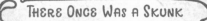

For this story game, everyone sits in a circle. If you're the first player, start by saying, "There once was a skunk who . . ." and finish the sentence by adding whatever words you like. After that sentence, you pass the story to someone else. This can be done with a ball or some other throwable object if you want to "throw" the story around, or you can simply go around the circle left to right or right to left.

The next person to add to the story begins the sentence with "Unfortunately . . ." And then the next person starts the next sentence with "Fortunately . . ." The story continues going around the circle until it's complete or until nobody can think of anything to add. You can stop anytime you like. Here's an example of how the story could unfold:

Player 1: There once was a skunk who liked to eat flowers.

Player 2: Unfortunately, flowers made him sick.

Player 3: Fortunately, whenever he got sick, his friends brought him gifts.

Player 4: Unfortunately, the gifts were always flowers.

And so on and so on . . .

For this game, you'll need some paper, a pen, and tape. First, have everyone take a small piece of paper and secretly write down a person, place, or thing. Write down anything that comes to mind, from the name of the street you live on to your favorite fruit.

Next, find someone to swap with. Without showing what you've written, tape the pieces of paper to each other. They should be placed somewhere where others can see them but the person they're taped to can't, so attach them to your backs or even on your foreheads. Just decide what works best. Once everyone has their "identities" stuck in place, you're ready to play.

Now the players have to figure out their identities without looking at what the pieces of paper stuck to them say. To do this, they can ask "yes" and "no" questions.

As players collect answers, they'll be able to ask more and more specific questions. Take turns asking questions and see how many questions it takes to correctly guess who or what you are.

Here are the kinds of questions you can ask to help you figure it out:

Am I a person?

Am I an animal?

Am I a place?

Can I be eaten?

Am I alive?

Do I live outside?

Am I sour?

Do I have hair?

Once when we were playing "What Am I?" the name written on Eugene's piece of paper was "Eugene." But for the life of him, he could not guess his own identity! Poor Eugene. He really doesn't know himself at all!

Games on the Go

My friends and I like getting out and exploring the forest in and around Corona. There are lots of neat games that are perfect to play when you're on the go, since all you need is friends to play with and a little imagination! Of course, for now our little trips are all inside the walls of the kingdom, but one day soon I'm hoping to explore beyond them. And when I do, these on-the-go games will help make the time fly by.

For a simple game of "Name That Tune," hum a few notes of a song and see how long it takes your friends to guess what song it is. Give them only a few notes at first, and if they are unable to guess it, give them a few more. See how many notes they need to figure out the song you're humming.

Or play a songwriting game. Name a subject and then listen as your friend makes up a song about it. Once that song is done, your friend gives you a topic, and you try your own hand at songwriting.

PUNCH SLUGGY

In this game, you keep your eyes open as you look for slugs. If you spot one, you get to playfully punch another player in the arm while shouting "Punch Sluggy!"

This is one of Cassandra's favorite games—she especially likes playing it against Eugene. But she does tend to take the term *playfully* to a whole new level when she slugs him!

CLAP IT OUT

Hand-clapping games are fun when you need a little break on the road. There are many hand-clapping games people share, but making up your own is also fun. Add a little rhyme or a song to your routine for an added challenge.

Here are some basic hand-clapping moves to incorporate in your routine:

1 Clap the palms of your hands together.

2 Clap the palms of your hands against your friend's palms.

3 Slap your thighs.

4 Cross your arms and tap your shoulders.

5 Clap the palm of your left hand against your friend's right hand.

6 Put both hands together and hold them vertically. Swipe them against your friend's hands.

7 Clap the backs of your hands against the backs of your friend's hands.

8 Put your right palm facing down and your left facing up. Your friend does the opposite so you can slap your palms together up and down.

9 Snap your fingers.

10 Spread your palms and fingers out and freeze.

Exploring to Find Adventure

'With my new freedom, 'I just can't stop exploring this amazing world that's all around me! 'Now there's exploring and then there's exploring to find adventure. 'But you can't find adventure when you're just sitting around. 'So get out there! 'Be brave and let your explorations lead you to new and exciting experiences you never even dreamed of!

Track your adventures by making your own map. Draw streams, hills, large boulders, and other landmarks. Highlight the path you hiked and decorate the map with details.

Try showing a "secret special spot" on the map—give a designated rock or tree a name (like Flat Rock or Old Hollow Tree) and draw a map leading someone to it. See if your friends can follow your map and find your secret special spot! If you have a compass, use it to help make your map.

I learned about poisonous plants the hard way–ouch!
Just the thought of it still makes me feel itchy and splotchy all
over. But Cassandra has some helpful tips to avoid them.

CASSANDRA'S POISONOUS PLANT TIPS

So, the worst poisonous plants are the ones that brush up against you and leave an itchy red rash behind. I like to think of them the same way I think of obstacles. Here's my simple rule for avoiding them: If there's a path, stay on it. If you're going off the beaten path—which Raps and I love doing, by the way—you really need to keep an eye out for those nasty plants. And no matter which path you're on or off, wearing long pants and shirts with long sleeves really helps. Have you ever heard this helpful rhyme? "Leaves of three, let it be." It's a good little guide, but don't go touching that plant just because it doesn't have three leaves. There are plenty of poisonous plants out there to watch out for, which is why it's a good idea to do some research before hiking in a new area. But here are three pretty common ones:

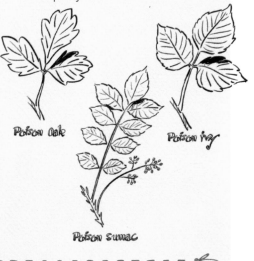

Poison Oak

Poison Ivy

Poison Sumac

There are plenty of plants and berries in nature that look tempting to eat. But take it from me, just don't. Many plants are poisonous, so you should never grab something off a tree or a bush and pop it in your mouth unless you're 100 percent sure that it's edible. My advice: stick to those snacks you packed and you'll be better off.

I hate to say it, but wearing comfortable shoes makes it easier to get around. I myself am not a big fan of shoes in general, but Cassandra swears they're important. So now I always wear sturdy shoes when we head out on an adventure. Also, always bring plenty of water and a few snacks. It's no fun if your adventure has to be cut short because of a rumbling tummy!

COMPASS GAMES

Set up a treasure hunt using a compass and a map. First, hide treasures (they can be seashells, coins, or whatever you like). Keep track as you hide each treasure and set a starting point. Then write down the directions using the compass. For example, "Start at the Old Hollow Tree. Walk fifteen paces at sixty degrees." Make sure you have the starting point right—draw a simple chart or map to help. Then make sure the directions to the next treasure start at the previous one.

You can also play hide-and-go-seek with your compass. First, find a starting place and have your friends close their eyes. Then use the compass to chart your path to a hiding spot. Write the instructions, and when you are done, leave them and the compass by your friends' feet.

Next, tell them to count to fifty with their eyes closed while you go to the hiding spot. When they open their eyes, they can use the compass and your chart to try to find you.

Go hiking at night and see how different everything looks under the stars. Bring a friend or two and take a source of light like a lantern to help you get around. It's a good idea to bring a blanket, too. Then hike out to a spot you like, take a seat on your blanket, and open your eyes and ears to see what new things the night brings.

Wait a minute. Stars! What could be better than ending your day with a little stargazing? Let's go!

Stars aren't only beautiful to look at. The stars can also help you find your way. On a clear night, you can find the North Star to tell you which way north is.

Stargazing

Stars are incredible, aren't they? I mean, I thought they were amazing from the tower, where I could only see a small section of sky. But once I was free and looked up at the night sky for the first time . . . I couldn't believe how many stars and constellations there were up in that great big beautiful sky. I love looking up and seeing a million twinkling lights–I can't help thinking of them as floating lanterns, way off in the distance.

One of the easiest stars to see is the North Star. To spot it, you'll have to find the "Frying Pan." Okay, so some people call it the Big Dipper, but either way this constellation will help you find north. The Frying Pan is made up of seven stars. Find the two stars of the  pan's edge farthest from its handle and draw a line up until you find a very bright star. That's the North Star! The North Star also helps make up the handle of the "Mini Frying Pan," also known as the Little Dipper.

Eugene thought this constellation looked like his eyebrows. He named it "Brows of Mine" even though it's actually called Cassiopeia.

Try to look for stars on a clear night and seek out the darkest place you can find. (If there are lots of lights around, the stars are more difficult to see.) A beach, a park, or a clearing in the forest are all perfect spots for star spotting.

Bring a blanket, sit down, and keep your eyes on the sky. It might take a little while for your eyes to adjust. You might even glimpse a shooting star.

Learn a few constellations before you go stargazing, or just connect the dots and make up your own.

Cass didn't name this constellation, but she got a kick out of finding this bow and arrow in the sky. Its official name is the Archer.

STAR MAP

Make a star map of the constellations you and your friends find. Then bring it with you on another clear night and try to find the same constellations again.

You can use a black piece of paper and white paint to make your star map look more like a real nighttime sky.

Moon gazing can be just as much fun as stargazing. I love looking up at the moon's craters and seeing the pictures they create on the surface. My favorite kind of moon is full and bright, the kind of moon that lights up the night sky, showing off the big beautiful world we live in.